Trouble

WRITTEN BY **Jane Kurtz**

ILLUSTRATED BY **Durga Bernhard**

GULLIVER BOOKS

HARCOURT BRACE & COMPANY

San Diego   New York   London

Library of Congress Cataloging-in-Publication Data
Kurtz, Jane.
Trouble/written by Jane Kurtz; illustrated by Durga Bernhard.
p.   cm.
"Gulliver Books."
Summary: A retelling of a traditional Eritrean tale in which a
young goatherd disobeys his father by trading away the board game
that was supposed to keep him out of trouble.
ISBN 0-15-200219-7
[1. Folklore—Eritrea.]   I. Bernhard, Durga, ill.   II. Title.
PZ8.1.K9854Tr 1997
398.2'09635—dc20
[E]   95-39308

Printed in Singapore
First edition
A C E F D B

The illustrations in this book were done in Winsor & Newton
gouache on Whatman 140-lb. cold-press watercolor paper.
The text type was set in Bernhard Gothic Heavy.
The display type was set in Goudy Sans Black.
This book was printed on totally chlorine-free Nymolla Matte Art paper.
Color separations by Rainbow Graphics, Singapore
Printed and bound by Tien Wah Press, Singapore
Production supervision by Stanley Redfern and Pascha Gerlinger
Designed by Durga Bernhard and Lydia D'moch

For Daniel and Lily Yohannes
and Abinet Haile,
good roommates and friends
with roots in three countries
—J. K.

For Kalifa Sissoko
—D. B.

Trouble always found Tekleh. When he ran by the fire, he never meant to kick dust onto the coffee beans roasting there. But somehow dust settled onto the beans just the same.

When Tekleh watched the family goats, he always meant to tend them carefully. How was it the goats so often ended up in someone else's garden?

And Tekleh could never resist poking a stick into a marching line of army ants to watch them climb on it. Was it his fault if the ants sometimes climbed up the stick and stung his fingers?

Finally, one day, Tekleh's father took a piece of olive wood and carefully hollowed out holes to make a *gebeta* board. "Now we will have no more problems," he told the family. "A *gebeta* board always keeps a young boy out of trouble." That evening, Tekleh and his father played the game together, scooping pebbles first into one hole and then another.

The next morning, Tekleh set off with two goats and his *gebeta* board. "Take the goats straight to their grazing place in the hills," his father reminded him. "You can play your game there with the other shepherds."

"Yes, Father," Tekleh said. And he meant to go straight to the hills. But as he began to walk, he could see, far in the distance, that something was happening on the path.

When Tekleh got closer, he saw it was a group of traders, with their dusty, musky camels, drinking coffee around a small fire. "Is there no wood in this country?" one of the traders called to Tekleh. "We found only a few sticks to make this fire."

"Of course there is wood," Tekleh said. "See?" And he held up his *gebeta* board.

"Thank you," the man said. He grabbed the *gebeta* board and threw it on the fire.

When Tekleh saw his *gebeta* board burning, he set up such a howling that the traders had to cover their ears. *"Aiieee!"* one cried. "Have this fine knife and stop that noise."

Well, Tekleh was still sad about his *gebeta* board, but the knife was sharp, with a strong bone handle. If the man had misunderstood him, what could be done now? So down the path Tekleh went with his two goats and the fine knife.

Before long, Tekleh saw a man sitting by the long grass, waiting. So he squatted and waited too.

"Here," the man said. "A knife is no thing for a young boy. Why don't you let me have it so I can skin the dik-dik that will soon be caught in my snare?"

Now, Tekleh had many times sat watching the dik-dik eating, *zik zik*, in the long grass. He was sorry to think of such a shy and delicate animal becoming a meal, but he knew people must eat. So he said, "What will you give me if I give you this fine knife?"

The man held out his *masinko*. "My family needs food more than they need music," he said.

So off Tekleh went with his two goats and his *masinko*. He wandered down the path, moving the bow this way and that to make sounds come from the instrument. About noon, he heard shouting up ahead. Soon he came upon a group of musicians dressed in fine clothes, strutting and shaking their shoulders as they danced.

"Here," one of the musicians said. "What a terrible noise you're making with that *masinko*. Why don't you let us have it for the wedding feast we're going to? You take this drum instead."

"Why not?" Tekleh said. But instead of turning toward the hills with his two goats and his drum, Tekleh tagged along after the musicians. At a wedding feast, Tekleh knew, a small boy can always be well fed from plates of leftovers.

Soon the group reached the house where the bride and groom and their guests celebrated. The red smell of spices curled in the air. In the middle of the thumping drums and dancing people, no one noticed Tekleh dipping his fingers in the pots and sampling the food. Finally one of the cooks chased him away. Full of the delicious wedding feast, Tekleh set off down the road with his goats and his drum.

The sun was hot and the air was sweet with the smells of grain and flowers. Tekleh stopped to watch an emerald lizard sunning itself on a rock. True, his mother always told him not to touch lizards. But this lizard sat on the rock so mysterious and still that Tekleh could not resist. He popped it into his bag to take home to eat flies and mosquitoes in the house.

A little while later, when the afternoon sun became too hot, Tekleh sat down in the shade of a cornfield and began to play his drum. Startled by the noise, three monkeys leaped out of the corn and scampered away, hooting. As the monkeys ran away from his fields, the farmer came running over to Tekleh. "What a wonderful noise," the farmer exclaimed. "Stay here and play your drum all afternoon, and I will give you a bag full of corn."

So Tekleh sat on the farmer's platform and played the drum to keep the monkeys and birds away, while the goats grazed on *mashella* tassles.

When the early evening shadows crawled across the ground, Tekleh gave the drum to the farmer in exchange for a fat papaya. Then Tekleh took his corn, his goats, his papaya, and his lizard and started for home.

But at the edge of his village, the smells of a cook fire caught him. "Salaam," called a woman from the doorway of her house. "Where did you get the fat papaya? I would like to get one for my children, who have been sick."

"A farmer gave it to me, but he is quite a long way from here," Tekleh replied. He looked at the children staring up at him with big, sad eyes. The youngest girl smiled shyly. "Here," Tekleh said. "Let me make you a gift of this bag of corn and the papaya."

"Come in, come in," the woman said. She blew on the fire under a pot of lentils and filled a bowl for Tekleh. While he scooped up the smoky lentils with his *injera*, he watched the children playing with their *gebeta* board. The woman cut the papaya, and the children ate it with juice running down their arms. Then Tekleh coaxed the goats out of the neighbor's garden to eat the leftover skin and seeds, said good-bye, and started down the path. Suddenly he heard footsteps. The littlest girl was running after him, holding out the *gebeta* board.

So it was that Tekleh came home with two goats, one emerald lizard, and a *gebeta* board.

His father patted Tekleh on the head with pride. "How well fed and contented the goats are today!" Tekleh's father said to the family. "Did I not tell you? A *gebeta* board never fails to keep a young boy out of trouble."

A NOTE ABOUT THE STORY

This story of a little boy and his *gebeta* board was one I heard as a child growing up in Ethiopia. When I decided to write my own version, I used my memories of the shepherd boys who cared for their cows and goats and sheep on the hills around our house. I also used a bit of myself. Somehow, when I was a little girl, I never could resist sticking a twig into those lines of marching ants, and though the Ethiopian adults around me told me not to handle things like frogs and lizards—because many people believed the animals caused certain diseases—I played with frogs constantly and was determined to catch one of the lizards that slid down our tin roof with a scraping sound.

A version of this folktale was collected by Harold Courlander and included in his book *Fire on the Mountain* (Henry Holt, 1950). Because Courlander heard the story in Eritrea, I decided it would be right to set my story there.

When I was a child, Eritrea was part of Ethiopia. I didn't realize when my family visited Eritrea that people in that part of the country were fighting for independence from Ethiopia—a fight that lasted thirty years. In the 1980s, the war became very intense and many people suffered. Finally, in April 1993, Eritrea became an independent country.

Eritrea is like Ethiopia in many ways. The countries' peoples wear similar clothes, eat similar foods, and live in similar ways. But Eritrea's history is quite different from Ethiopia's. Eritrea has a seacoast along the Red Sea and, unlike Ethiopia, was an Italian colony from 1889 to 1941. Today there are adults in Eritrea who never knew life without war until now. The war has left thousands of its inhabitants hungry and displaced. But most visitors to Eritrea come away impressed by the people's determination, hope, and hard work. Now that Eritreans can walk and work and play safely in the daylight, perhaps Eritrea will again someday be a place where a little boy and his goats can wander and not get into too much trouble.

—Jane Kurtz

GLOSSARY

 dik-dik (dik-dik):
a very small antelope

 **gebeta (GUH-buh-tuh):**
a popular board game played all over the world, also called mancala

 injera (in-JE-rah):
a large, spongy pancake used as bread at most meals in Eritrea and Ethiopia

 mashella (mah-SHULL-ah):
sorghum, a grass grown for its grain

 masinko (mah-SINK-oh):
a one-stringed fiddle with a diamond-shaped sound box, a thick horsehair string, and a curved wooden bow

 Tekleh (TUK-kuh-luh):
literally translated as "to plant"